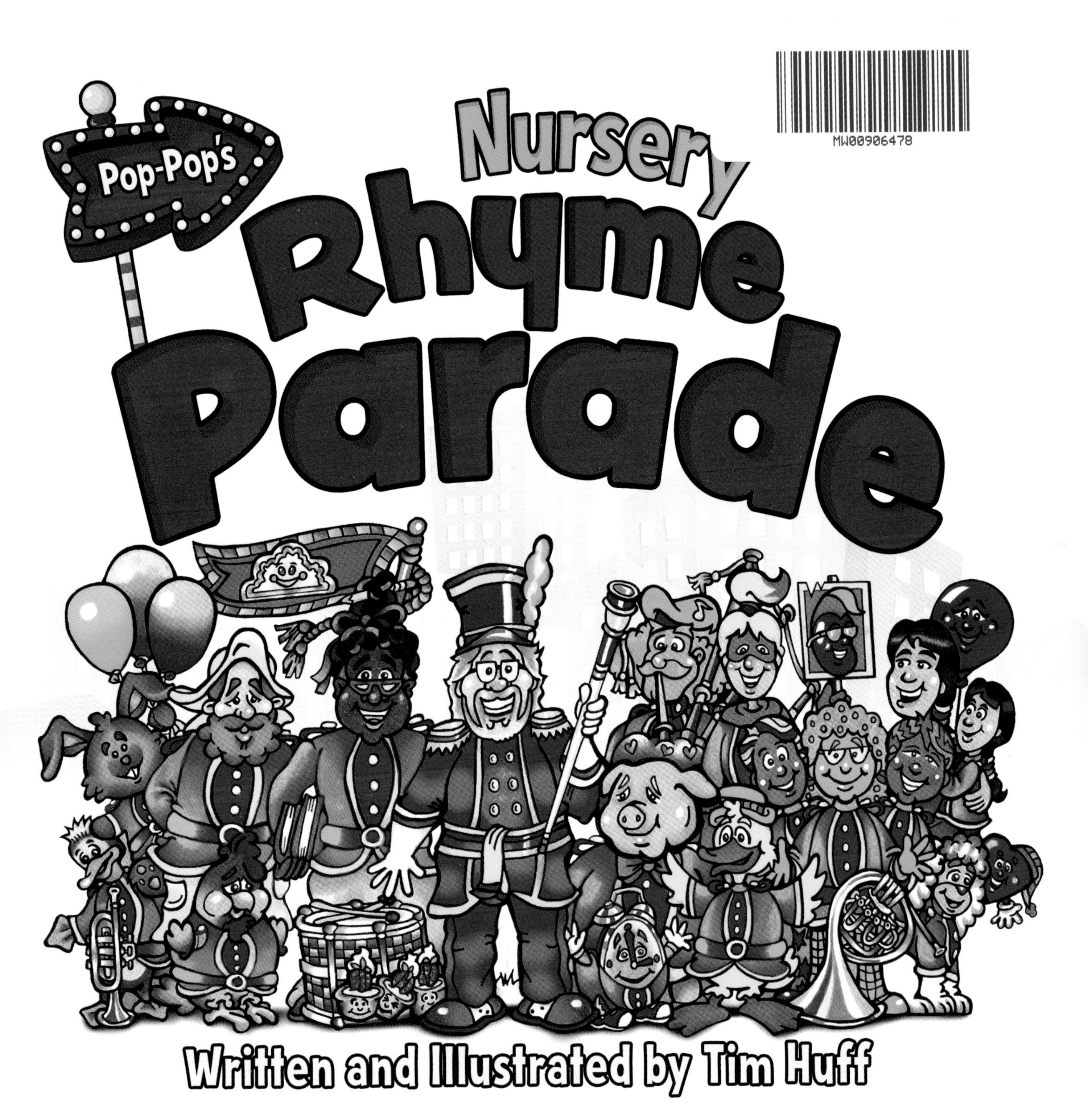
MW00906478
Pop-Pop's
Nursery
Rhyme
Parade
Written and Illustrated by Tim Huff

POP-POP'S NURSERY RHYME PARADE

978-1-988928-86-9 Soft Cover
978-1-988928-87-6 E-book

Published by:
Castle Quay Books
Burlington, Ontario
Tel: (416) 573-3249
E-mail: info@castlequaybooks.com | www.castlequaybooks.com

Edited by Marina Hofman Willard
Cover and internal Illustrations by Tim J. Huff
Cover and book interior design by Burst Impressions
Printed in Canada.

Library and Archives Canada Cataloguing in Publication
Title: Pop-Pop's nursery rhyme parade / written and illustrated by Tim J. Huff.
Other titles: Nursery rhyme parade
Names: Huff, Tim, 1964- author, illustrator.
Description: Series statement: Compassion series | Includes bibliographical references and index.
Identifiers: Canadiana (print) 20240325621 | Canadiana (ebook) 2024032563X | ISBN 9781988928869 (softcover) | ISBN 9781988928876 (EPUB)
Subjects: LCGFT: Picture books. | LCGFT: Poetry.
Classification: LCC PS8615.U3145 P66 2024 | DDC jC811/.6—dc23

A Message from Pop-Pop to the Grownups

Until I was about ten, I went by Timmy. I have also been Timothy and T.J. at different times among different folks. But for most of my life, and to most people, I have simply been Tim.

But something magical happened when I became Pop-Pop—a name I was gifted upon the arrival of my first grandchild. All of a sudden, both the little world I inhabited and the big world all around me looked and felt very—very—different.

I recall a similar experience when I became Daddy for the first time, but things felt different then. During that moment of newness in my life, society didn't seem quite so perplexing, and technology was not as intrusive and didn't advance at the speed we witness today.

I have authored and co-authored books that explore many complex topics and invite important conversations for both children and adults. Yet in many ways, for me personally, this gentle and cheerful book of poetry for children feels the most vital. No doubt, while writing and illustrating it, I felt a bit of the young Timmy in me looking on. More than that, as Pop-Pop, I felt an overwhelming ache for ideas, words, and phrases filled with innocence, gentleness, and joy—at a time when they seem too rare. From the earnest longing of this grandfather's heart, I created these poems and pictures, praying that they may be both a timely offering and a timeless one.

My hope is for the heart of this book to beat in time with the heartbeat of every safe and loving parent, grandparent, and loved one to a child. And for it to provide a few fun chuckles and happy messages for teachers to share in their classrooms.

In previous book introductions, I have written about the inherent risk of putting words on paper: that as meanings and nuances in language change over generations and with sweeping cultural shifts, the words here in print remain fixed in time. And so, even here, I simply remain prayerful and hopeful that the spirit of this book is never lost, whatever the future holds.

Please know, *Pop-Pop's Nursery Rhyme Parade* is written and illustrated by someone who is greatly humbled by the passing of time, by both the wild unpredictability and routine day-to-dayness of life, and God's grace in it all. Be assured that this author and illustrator has an intentionally attentive heart toward those who walk paths much different to my own.

Whoever you are, I am so grateful you're holding this book in your hands. My heart fully believes that you and the children in your life are cherished by a loving God—this is a truth I am careful not to hide and am also compelled to pair with the assurance that there is no agenda here. There is only a humble hope that these nursery rhymes bring a measure of comfort, joy, and goodness to you and the children in your home, school, or community.

Peace and all the very best,

Pop-Pop

Pop-Pop

Strawberry Tartlets

Strawberry tartlets—one, two, three.
Oh, but you look so good to me.
Waiting until my supper ends.
Waiting for me to bring two friends.

But what if they were all for me?
If I could have all one, two, three?
Would that be best, would that be wise?
If I ate all three tiny pies?

Think and think and think I do.
Think until my dinner's through.
Think of tartlets—oh so sweet.
And of the friends that I could treat.

Finally, now my dinner's done.
Here they come—yum, yum, yum.
Strawberry tartlets—one, two, three.
Two to share and one for me.

Bunnies Don't Run

Bunnies don't run.
They hop, hop, hop.

Ponies don't skip.
They trot, trot, trot.

When birds fly high, the fish don't care.
'Cause everyone's different, everywhere.

Carrots don't smoosh.
They CRUNCH, CRUNCH, CRUNCH.

Bananas only grow
in a bunch, bunch, bunch.

If the berries taste sweet, the beans don't care.
'Cause everyone's different, everywhere.

Oceans don't trickle.

They roar, roar, roar.

Waves roll into
the shore, shore, shore.

If the rivers run wild, the ponds don't care.
'Cause everyone's different, everywhere.

If people were all the same, same, same,
That would be such a shame, shame, shame.
Love them all and say a prayer
For everyone different, everywhere.

Maybe I'll Bounce

Maybe I'll bounce on puffy clouds
And chat with the friendly sun.
Maybe I'll ride on a shooting star.
Maybe on more than one.

Maybe I'll dine with a porcupine
And play with a big brown bear.
Maybe I'll dance with a platypus.
Maybe even with a pair.

Maybe I'll go where no one's been,
No other boy or girl.
Maybe I'll discover something new.
Maybe I'll change the world.

Maybe for now I'll just stay here
And dream of the things I'll do.
'Cause maybe the best thing I'll ever know
Is the time that I spend with you.

One Grumpy Hour

One grumpy hour—tick, tick, tock.
Just one hour—it's all I've got.
One grumpy hour to huff and puff,
Just one hour, then "enough's enough."

Sometimes I pout; sometimes I frown.
Sometimes I stomp with my head hung down.
I don't need a fuss when I feel sour.
All I need is one grumpy hour.

A little rest and quiet time,
A while alone and I'll be fine.
An honest "sorry" and a little chat,
A happy hug and then that's that.

One grumpy hour—tick, tick, tock.
Just one hour—it's all I've got.
One grumpy hour to huff and puff,
Just one hour, then "enough's enough."

Jellybean Rockstar

Jellybean Rockstar
Do your thing
All you jellybeans, sing, sing, sing

Jellybean Pilot
In the sky
All you jellybeans, fly, fly, fly

Jellybean Diver
Jump right in
All you jellybeans, swim, swim, swim

Jellybean Farmer
Grow things big
All you jellybeans, dig, dig, dig

Jellybean Teacher
Pen and ink
All you jellybeans, think, think, think

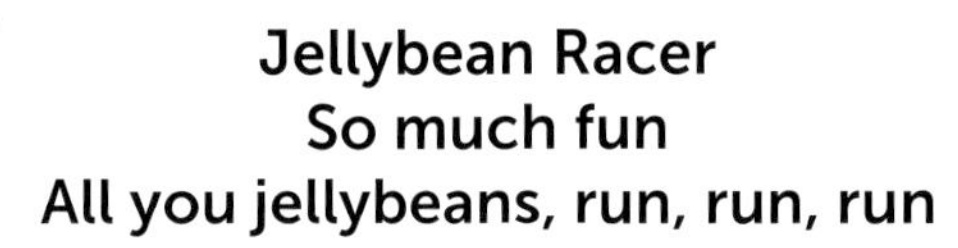

Jellybean Racer
So much fun
All you jellybeans, run, run, run

Jellybean, Jellybean
You and me
Imagine everything we can be

My Little Nightlight

My little nightlight is my best friend.
Not in the day, but when the day ends.
Just enough warmth, just enough glow,
Just enough light to let me know ...

I am safe. I'm okay.
It's all right to drift away
To happy sleep, without fear,
Knowing those I love are near.

Bedtime for Mr. Sunshine

It's bedtime for Mr. Sunshine,
bedtime for Grandma Jane,

Bedtime for Uncle Wallaby
who likes fishing in the rain.

It's bedtime for Aunt Augustine
who sure knows how to **snore**,

Bedtime for Tommy Wigglesworth
who tends the corner store.

It's bedtime for my teacher.
I'm guessing that she sleeps?

Bedtime for the farmers,
the chickens and the sheep.

It's bedtime for the puppy
we played with at the park,

Bedtime for the flowers
out sleeping in the dark.

It's bedtime for my slippers
and for my teddy bear,

It's bedtime, so it's the best time, to say my bedtime prayer ...

Now I pray for sweet, sweet dreams

Of white fluffy clouds over bright blue streams.

Of plump red apples on tall green trees

And high-flying kites on a soft warm breeze.

For mommies to laugh and daddies to smile,

Just watching the children play for a while.

Of breakfast at eight and lunchtime at noon,

And ol' Mr. Sunshine coming back to us soon.

Lullaby for Mommy

Sleep now, Mommy, and dream sweet dreams
Of gentle, happy days.
Know, dear Mommy, how much I know
The never-ending ways
You give and give and give again,
Always thinking of
How to keep me safe and warm
And fill our home with love.

Sleep now, Mommy, and I will stay
So very close to you.
And while you sleep, I will think
Of everything you do.
And if tears come to my eyes,
It will only be
Because my heart knows so well
How much you mean to me.

Drummer Jan and Bagpipe Bob

Drummer Jan and Bagpipe Bob
Finally got a music job.

Drummer Jan to rat-tat-tat,
Bagpipe Bob to play B-flat.

B-flat on the pipes is tough
And drumming isn't easy stuff.

And so they practised all day long
A very, very simple song.

Just B-flat and rat-tat-tat
Until they'd had enough of that.

There was still so much to do,
Something more, something new.

Tomorrow they would have to start
A tough tap-tap and a hard G-sharp.

The Muckity Muck

There once was a duck named Lucky.
Lucky was a lucky duck.
He had a pal named Mucky;
A pig from a muckity muck.

Now Lucky and Mucky had a friend named Bill.
Bill was a kangaroo.
A kangaroo with eyes of blue
And purple and yellow running shoes.

And Bill had a sister named Tillie.
Bill used to call her Till.
Till would say she would play all day
If she could only find a way.

So Bill and Till went a-walking
Down to the muckity muck.
There they knew they would have some luck
Finding a pig and a lucky duck.

Lucky and Mucky were laughing
When Bill and Till jumped in.
But they played too long and they stayed too long.
Then one cried out, “Something’s wrong!”

The sun was hot and bright that day
And the soft mud would not stay that way
So they wiggled and jiggled till they got loose—
A duck, a pig and some kangaroos.

So remember Lucky and Mucky.
And think of Bill and Till
If you’re out of luck and you get stuck,
Playing too long in the muckity muck.

Rosie was a red balloon
At the county fair.
Billie was a blue balloon
Floating through the air.

When Rosie saw Billie fly,
She looked down at her string.
"Why is she a sky balloon?
And I'm a different thing."

But when she saw the little girl
Holding on to her,
She remembered something good,
Something that felt sure.

Some of us are meant for skies,
Some are meant for play.
Some balloons are best to fly,
Some are best to stay.

Red balloons and blue balloons,
Be what you will be.
Just remember you bring joy
To everyone you see.

Oodles of Poodles

Oodles of poodles went for a walk,
As oodles of poodles will do.
Ev'ry one barked as they strolled through the park.
Just why, nobody knew.

Oodles of poodles got to the river,
As oodles of poodles will do.
They all jumped in to go for a swim;
The water was icy and blue.

Oodles of poodles got back to the shore,
As oodles of poodles will do.
They shivered and quivered, there at the river.
Their little adventure was through.

Oodles of poodles ran back to their home,
As oodles of poodles will do.
All so tired, they sat by the fire.
Of course, now, wouldn't you?

So if you see oodles of poodles,
And wonder, "What should I do?"
Run to the river so you can deliver
A big cozy towel or two.

Skedaddle

Sometimes I have to skedaddle.
Skedaddle, lickety-split.
No, I won't dilly-dally
Or lollygag, even a bit.

Sometimes I'm a flibbertigibbet
When I see a hullaballoo.
I'm happy when a kerfuffle
Turns into a whoop-da-de-doo.

Sometimes I can razzle-dazzle
When I have a thingamabob.
If I don't get bamboozled,
I can do a jolly good job.

So if you have to skedaddle
Away from a hullaballoo,
Don't forget your thingamabob,
And now you know what to do.

Superhero, Oh Please Be

Superhero, oh please be
Superhero STRONG.

Superhero, do your best
If you see things are wrong.

Superhero, oh please be
Superhero kind.

Superhero, choose to stay
So no one's left behind.

Superhero, oh please be
Superhero **good**.

Superhero, do the things
That you know you should.

Superhero, oh please be
Superhero **smart**.

Superhero, don't forget
The love that's in your **HEART**.

Whatever May Happen

For mommies, daddies, grandparents, and safe loved ones —you are invited to insert the name you are affectionately known as where it reads "**Pop-Pop**".

Pop-Pop thanks God for you, every day.
And for every chance that we get to play.
Hearing you laugh, seeing you grow,
Brings ***Pop-Pop*** more joy than you'll ever know.

Pop-Pop is proud of you, year after year.
Pop-Pop cares deeply, tear after tear.
Whatever may happen, whatever may change,
Know ***Pop-Pop's*** love will always remain.

Pop-Pop is near and ***Pop-Pop*** will pray,
Through all of the tough stuff and every hard day,
For God to protect and heaven to bring
Laughter and love and every good thing.

Don't Forget the Music and Art!

What a joy to have some of *Pop-Pop's Nursery Rhyme Parade* set to music!

Some of Pop-Pop's dearest friends are extremely gifted musicians. And more than just super talent, they have tender hearts and joyous ways, infusing character and meaning into all their great musical endeavours. It's such a wonderful gift to have their special performances as part of the nursery rhyme parade experience.

To hear some of your favourite new nursery rhymes set to music by award-winning artists—including internationally acclaimed singer-songwriter Steve Bell and renowned pianist-composer-performer Mike Janzen—visit **compassionseries.com/music**.

And hey, there is still even more fun! For *Pop-Pop's Nursery Rhyme Parade* colouring and activity pages, visit **compassionseries.com/colour**.

Tim Huff, aka Pop-Pop

Tim has dedicated his adult life to full-time charitable work, serving, learning, and teaching across North America and internationally. Throughout his career, he has combined his passion for visual arts, writing, and music with his commitment to social justice and compassion-focused initiatives. Recognized as an acclaimed speaker, Tim is also an award-winning author-illustrator of children's books and a best-selling author of books for adults.

His impressive track record of service and leadership includes serving as the staff director at the Ontario Camp of the Deaf and founding director roles at both Toronto's Frontlines Youth Centre and Youth Unlimited's Light Patrol street outreach. Tim has been the driving force behind Youth Unlimited's Compassion Series program—a unique and innovative hub providing creative and interactive compassion-focused resources for children, youth, families, and classrooms.

COMPASSION SERIES BOOKS FOR CHILDREN BY TIM HUFF AND FRIENDS

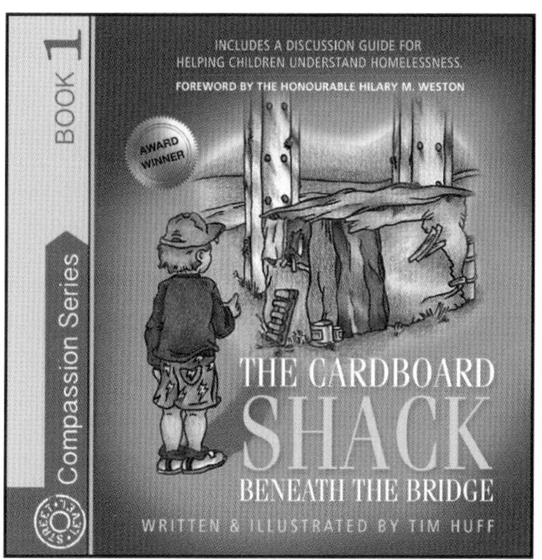

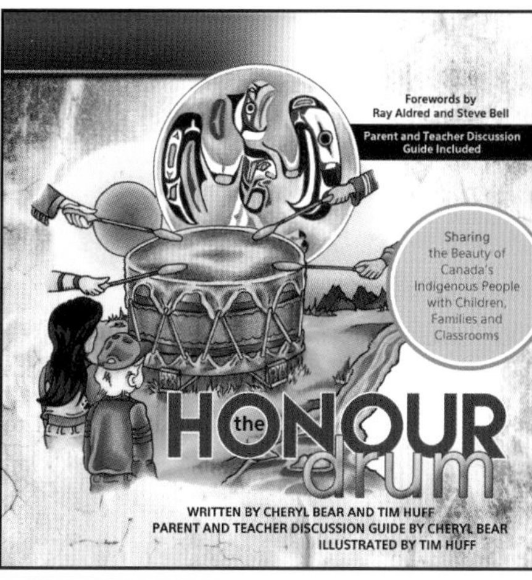

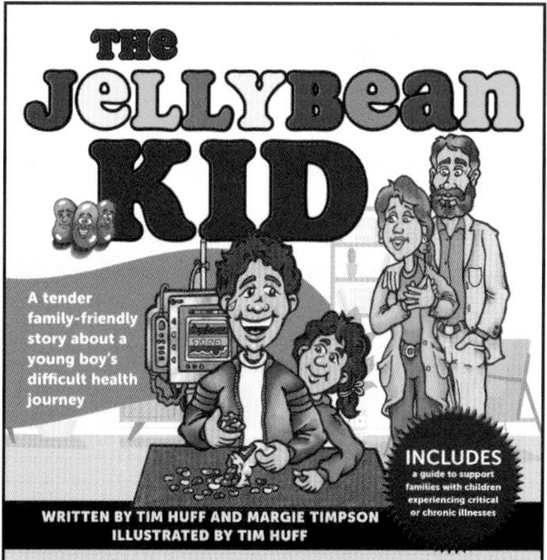

Find all of Tim's books for kids, teenagers and adults as well as audio books at compassionseries.com/books.